To Jodie – K. N.
To my mum – A. A.

First published 2018 by Nosy Crow Ltd, The Crow's Nest
14 Baden Place, Crosby Row, London SE1 1YW
www.nosycrow.com

ISBN 978 1 78800 098 7 (HB)
ISBN 978 1 78800 099 4 (PB)

Nosy Crow and associated logos are trademarks
and/or registered trademarks of Nosy Crow Ltd.

Text © Karl Newson 2018
Illustrations © Anuska Allepuz 2018
The right of Karl Newson to be identified as the author and of Anuska Allepuz
to be identified as the illustrator of this work has been asserted.
A CIP catalogue record for this book is available from the British Library.

Printed in China
Papers used by Nosy Crow are made from wood
grown in sustainable forests.

1 3 5 7 9 8 6 4 2 (HB)
1 3 5 7 9 8 6 4 2 (PB)

A BEAR is a BEAR

(except when he's not)

Karl Newson &
Anuska Allepuz

nosy crow

A bear is a bear.
Except when he's not . . .

What would he be, if a bear forgot?

Why...
a bird, of course!

Perched in a nest,
wondering why he outgrew all the rest.

Wondering why he cannot fly . . .

Wondering why, with a heavy sigh,

"If I'm not a bird, then what am I?"

For a bear is a bear.
Except when he's not ...

What would he be, if a bear forgot?

Why...
a moose, of course!

Tall and slow, wondering,
"Why do antlers grow?"

Wondering why the grass tastes dry . . .
Wondering why – oh me, oh my –

"I'm NOT a moose – I don't know why.
I'm NOT a bird. So what am I?"

For a bear is a bear.
Except when he's not ...

What would he be, if a bear forgot?

Why...
a fox, of course!

Who likes to dance,

wondering why it's hard to prance.

Wondering why his steps are awry . . .

Wondering why, with a tear in his eye,

"I'm NOT a fox –
but I gave it a try.

I'm NOT a moose –
I don't know why.

I'm NOT a bird –
I cannot fly.

So what, oh what, oh WHAT am I?"

For a bear is a bear.
Except when he's not . . .
What would he be, if a bear forgot?

Why...
a squirrel, of course!

Quick and small,
wondering if he's going to fall.
Wondering why he climbed so high . . .
Wondering why, oh why, oh why!

"I'm NOT a squirrel –
they climb too high.

I'm NOT a fox –
but I gave it a try.

I'm NOT a moose –
I don't know why.

And I'm NOT a bird –
I cannot fly.

So what, oh what
on earth am I?"

You used to know!
But you forgot.
At least we know now what you're not.

You're very tired
and grumpy too!
But I know what you need to do.

Now curl up tight, and not a peep . . .
Close your eyes and go to sleep.

This is your cave and here's the thing –
hibernation lasts till spring!
So off to sleep – it's just December!
No wonder that you can't remember!

For a bear is a bear,
but this bear forgot!

It's time to wake up now...
Ready or not!

Knock! Knock! Knock!
Hello in there?

There you are!
        And you're a ...

...BEAR!